Hideaway

Hideaway

Beverly Taylor

Beckham

Publications Group, Inc.

Silver Spring

Published in the United States by
Beckham Publications Group, Inc.
P.O. Box 4066, Silver Spring, MD 20914
ISBN: 978-0-9984870-9-0

Dedicated with love
to my husband Joseph Taylor
and our sons Aaron and Dennis

Contents

Chapter One: Hideaway 1

Chapter Two: The Edwards 13

Chapter Three: How Hideaway Got Its Name 17

Chapter Four: Hideaway Peoples' Church 27

Chapter Five: Them Eight Houses 33

Chapter Six: The Greens 37

Chapter Seven: The Finches................................ 41

Chapter Eight: The Morrises 45

Chapter Nine: Ella Mae...................................... 53

Chapter Ten: The Reverend Theodore Lucus Showall....61

Chapter Eleven: Deacon Pearl 71

Chapter Twelve: Sister Basset 87

Chapter Thirteen: Me and Randell...................... 101

Acknowledgements

To Mark Kelly for his skillful knowledge and encouragement.

To Thelma Austin of Praise Press for her help and support.

To Barry Beckham of Beckham Publications Group, Inc.

Thank you for your patience, faith, and all the valuable help you have given me.

1

Hideaway

I remember just as good the mornin Maxine Edwards called me. I was sittin at my kitchen table drinkin coffee and readin my Bible like I do for I start my day, when the telephone got to ringin. You know that's how the devil work, he wait right good til you tryin to have some private time with God and he get to buttin in your bizness. I didn't want to get up and go in my livin room where the phone was restin on my little table next to the couch. But I was glad I did. That call stirred me up some kinda good.

I said, "Hello."

The lady on the other end said, "Good morning," talkin real proper at 8:30 in the mornin. "My name is Maxine Edwards."

I wanted to cuss right then. I knew that call was Pearl Ann's doin. We go to the hairdresser on the same day. She gave your number out to anybody sellin life insurance or them cyclopedias. Pearl Ann was always lookin for some kinda discount or prize for herself.

But right before I was set to use one of them four-letter words, Ms. Edwards said, "My parents lived in Hideaway a couple of doors down from you." I changed my mind and listened. She said, "My parents are Wilford and Barbara Jean Edwards; they left Hideaway and moved to South Carolina."

I was tryin to picture in my mind who they were, but it was slow comin. I said, "Oh yea" like I was right there with her.

Stil talkin, she said, "I publish books for a living; I love reading and writing stories about our people and our journeys or life stories."

"That's great," answerin back. I was stil waitin on a piece of something to help me recollect who they were.

"My parents are still doing what they love; both of them are planting and selling good vege-tables."

When she said that plantin part, it hit me quick. I knew who her Momma and her Daddy was. They were the ones who was growin their own vegetables for a livin and sellin them out the trunk of their car. But I didn't tell her that. I let her talk.

"They owned their own vegetable and fruit market."

"Ain't that something," I said.

Ms. Edwards said she wanted to come back here to see where it all began for her parents after they finished college. She said her parents remembered the close-knit community and the love they felt with members of the church but she wanted to know more so she was in town to see for herself. I didn't want to make up no lie on all us bein knit and close but I did think back to the love her parents showed to community folk.

Ms. Edwards said she was amazed when she finally found our little tiny community the other day. But the thing she said that stuck so deep up in my head was a big tree she saw that gave her the feelin she was welcome. I know bout that tree!

When I left fifteen years ago, there were people livin there but I didn't keep up with anybody. But Ms. Edwards, she found it bare. She said the church and pieces of each of them eight houses was stil there. I listened as she described how the trees and weeds and wild flowers was growin up together in, out and round them houses. To me that meant there was nobody left to gather up them weeds. Ms. Edwards said she just walked quietly and looked at all the beauty and imagined on her own what life could have been for the people who lived there. She said she was not scared but sensed a presence of somebody bein glad she was there.

"I knew then there was a story to tell that was hidden back up in those woods." That young lady said she was determined to find somebody from our little neighborhood. She went back to the nearest town, found Joe's Black Barber Shop and told people who she was related to and where they use to live. She showed them some pictures of her parents. They opened up then.

Her momma gave her a piece of paper with some names of people that lived in Hideaway. My name was on that list, Betteen Dour.

Whoever she talked to, remembered me. They told her, "Ms. Dour stil livin, and if anybody can tell you bout Hideaway, it would be her."

They told Ms. Edward how to get in touch with me. When the Lord want you found, you can't hide!

She didn't want to take up much of my time. So, she said, "May I come by and talk to you about what your life was like and what you remember about your neighbors when you lived there?"

I told her, "All I can give you is my memories, if you want that."

She laughed and said, "Yes ma'am, I would be honored."

That child really reminded me of her momma when she said that. Her momma was an educated woman and always talked nice to people.

"Do you mind if I record your memories?"

I told that child, "You can record and write all you want to. Baby you breathin new life on a little place where people lived. You the first as far as I know to ever ask bout our town."

We set the week and time when we was gon get started.

I was so excited. I cleaned and re-cleaned and cooked all I could to get ready for my memories meetin. She walked in and gave me a big hug.

I asked her where she wanted to sit. She saw where I had some paper and pencils sittin real neat on my kitchen table, so we sat there. I did that just in case she needed it. I asked her would she like something to drink or eat. I had a pot of navy beans and sausage on the stove with some sweet cornbread. She asked for some cold water. I brought her some with ice in one of my good glasses to drink out of.

Ms. Edwards took a good sip and went over some rules for how we was gondo this recordin and all. She asked me, "Could you please describe how you all would get to Hideaway? Then could you tell me about the first African Americans who were there? I would love for you to tell me what you remember about my parents. But most of all how that small community got to be called Hideaway and the church and the people who lived, struggled and thrived there."

"Now before I get to talkin let me say this one thing. Ain't no sense in me lyin. You might find some gaps in my story, those coulda been times when I was tendin to my bizness and I wasn't lookin to see what my neighbor was doin. I had a life too you know."

"That's fine, I understand. Please take your time and talk about what you remember. I'm in no rush."

That child didn't know, but that's just what I wanted to hear. I could talk bout what I knew and I could take my time doin it.

She smiled sweet like, that made me feel good. "Do you have any questions," she asked.

"Yea, I got one. What you gon do with these stories, after I tell them to you."

That Ms. Edwards took a sip of water, waited a minute then said, "I'd like to put these stories together and let the world know where you all lived and how you all struggled and survived as a community."

I thought for a minute, I didn't tell her what I was thinkin, cause some of what I'm gon say bout our Hideaway community tells bout some bodies sweetness, bout some bodies sadness and some I don't know what order it belongs in. I didn't have no more questions. I was ready to tell her my memories as best I could.

First off, Hideaway didn't sit on no main road, and wasn't no arrows tellin you where to go, and wasn't no welcome sign to greet you when you got there. You just had to know where you was goin. Comin from town you took Jeff-Ann Road goin east. You stayed on it til you ran clean out of road, and all you saw in front of you was some railroad tracks and trees that sat on the other side of them.

When you made up your mind you was gon cross those old tracks, you was greeted by a narrow skimpy road we called No-Name.

You stayed on No-Name and drove til you got to the only guide we had to let you know you was close to Hideaway. It was a big old, old tree, showin her age. We called her Mamma tree.

That's the one you saw. She would be standin there with her children and they children all growin out of her. They arms stretched out, strong and wide livin they own way, with moss that dangled like long gray hair from their elbows. She had hers and their big claw feet all round the bottom of her trunk that clung deep into the dirt at the foot of the road. Now you couldn't spend time lookin at her while you was driven cause you had to turn your wheel gently to the right that led you into Hideaway. The minute you made that turn some tall trees greeted you on both sides of that skinny road, bent all over, like an arch, kissin each other, like they was kin. Now, that lastway was made by a whole lotta feet walkin people who been mashin down on that old dirt for so long they made a path. When you drove up in there you had to creep slow and easy like you was a snake cause our road was curvy and narrow. Now if it was dark, Lord knows you had bet not be drunk or in a hurry, you'd tear your car all to pieces. But once you got behind those kissin trees, sat, eight houses and a church.

Ms. Edwards, I told you how to get to Hideaway. Now I'm gon tell you what I know bout our first start, bout your momma and daddy, the name Hideaway, bout me, bout my neighbors who came to be a part of me, and me a part of them, like family. To be able to go back in the pass is a mighty strong force. I've got these memories, some good, some bad some painful but they stil with me. I'm gon pass them on to you, for you to do something good with them.

You already know my first name is Betteen. You spell it the way you say it. My last name is just like the front door to your house except you spell it with one "o" and a "u." I don't know why that is, but it is.

Now I'm gon get started.

It's very important that you know how we got to Hideaway in the first place. Some might not want to hear bout slavery and the war but we have to stop there for a short time. I promise you I won't hold you there long.

The story was told to me, a small group of freed slaves was movin north from a plantation they lived and worked on in South Carolina after the war, this was round bout 1865 or so. Back then it wasn't safe for freed slaves to be walkin round everywhere. But as the story goes an old woman, they called her Ma Shoog, was travelin with them. After awhile she got tired and needed to sit. They knew they had to get off that road and the only place to rest was in them woods with them big trees. Now they say, Ma

Shoog was known for prayin real loud all the time. She was a deep spirited old woman. She would walk round durin the night and pray. Some said she would pray so til the sky would just lighten up with thunder. But I heard stories that people feared her. They said she had a way of lookin at things and seein what nobody else saw. So slaves respected her wisdom and did not want to go on without her. So, they stayed put right there in them woods. Ma Shoog rested long enough for a dream to come to her. She told the young folks "There was seeds planted on this land before we got here, we just stopped for a little while to plant some more. There will be more of us to come and work this rich land and live here but you all got to move on. I'm gon to stay and watch the seeds grow for a little while, til a wind comes and blows my way."

None of them questioned her as they sat close and quite that night.

Ma Shoog walked a little ways in the woods rubbin her hands across them big old trees and talked to God. For a while the folks could hear her sayin,

"Lord I wanna thank you for bringin me right here and now. I know my work is to wait and watch for those who wonder through here from time to time. But I'm askin God that you please protect those that came this far with me. Prepare them on they journey called life. God, them angels you got please dole out one to each one here tonight to guard them in the day and the night. Lord please be ahead of them, beside and inside of them Lord. Keep them through the good and the bad. Bless them God. I pray they will honor you all they days. Amen Amen!"

They say the sky opened up and a cool wind came in soft after her prayer.

Some claimed they saw Ma Shoog walkin round them in the night while they slept. They found Ma Shoog dead the next mornin. They buried her under the dirt close to her tree in those woods and headed north.

Ma Shoog was right; more of us did come, and lived, and worked and died and stil more came.

We got there round bout the early 1940s.

Now I'm gone move round a bit so you got to stay with me. We gone get back to how our community got to be called Hideaway but I want to tell you what I know bout your momma and daddy right quick.

2

The Edwards

We had two houses that folks came and settled in for a short while and then they moved on. The first house was where your momma and daddy lived in 102.

Now I'm gon tell this story like they wasn't no kin to you, cause I want you to spend time picturin in your head what I saw and picked up on bout the type of people they were. I hope that's alright with you. Mr. Edwards and his wife Barbara Jean and a big face dog, they had rented the house. It wasn't in the best of shape but them Edwards worked hard at makin it look real sweet on the inside and out.

Them two was always together. Every now and then Mr. Edwards or Brother Edwards as we called him in the church was always showin their love for one another. They would kiss in the middle of plantin something. He would take

Barbara Jean and hold her in his arms and tell her in front of who ever and say, "I love you girl".

She would smile up at him and shake her pretty head. But you talkin bout a woman workin, she hauled and carried plantin stuff just like him. Barbara Jean loved holdin dirt and lookin at it like it was a piece of gold she found. They knew we looked at them funny when they used all them long scientific names for every flower, weed and stitch of grass growin.

But they was educatin us to. They told us, they met each other at one of them black colleges in Florida. Both of them was in the same class lovin on weeds and bugs at the same time.

Ain't that something! They finished school, got married and moved to Hideaway. They both started plantin and growin they own vegetables on a little piece of land. The big farmers didn't take to them growin on their own cause they had the best lookin vegetables in the county. Plus they had schoolin to go long with it. Them Edwards grew and sold their best on the road or out of his trunk on Saturdays at the ball games and after church on Sunday.

One time the Sheriff wrote them up. They had the right papers to sell goods on the street but the sheriff said those laws don't apply to colored farmers. But they knew how to pray, have faith and press to see what the end would be. Mr. Edwards carried that gun and that big faced dog just in case. They were smart and young but most of all they believed in God and in each other. They never lost sight of their dreams of ownin their own vegetable market. But as much as they loved the rich soil they knew they had to sow seeds somewhere else. I believe Mr. Edwards said he had a brother who lived in South Carolina who lived on a piece of land that was big enough for his dream. He and Barbara Jean moved on down there to sow more seeds. You know with prayer and faith, I know they did just that!

Now I told you bout the Edwards, your momma and daddy. I got to stop right here and tell you how we got to live in Hideaway.

3

How Hideaway Got Its Name

Many of us worked for a white man name Cecil Hideaway.

We worked in his fields and in his house, day in and day out. He had a big peanut farm and just bout every stitch of land round it handed down to him from his father, Amus Hideaway.

Cecil learned from him how to run the farm and control the people who worked for him. He never knew his mother and whenever he asked his father bout her, he said, "I didn't need a wife I only wanted a son."

Well, Cecil loved his father and looked just like him too. He was a big tall man with big teeth and eyes that never seemed to keep stil. He wore white short sleeve shirts mostly and britches clean up to his chest with suspenders. He had a stomach that sat out in front of him. He walked the way a duck would waddle from side to side. He got his leg caught in a trap when he was a boy, it never got back straight. He had no hair on the top of his head but spent a lot of time pattin on the brown hair he did have.

Cecil didn't really play with children his age as a child cause his father always had him close under him. When his father died he was thirty years old and unmarried. Bein alone he knew he wanted children. So he found a young woman in her early twenties stil livin at home with her poor family. A woman who wouldn't be a bit more concern bout his high wasted britches or his big teeth. He didn't bother to ask her if she wanted to marry him. Mr. Cecil didn't ask the family no questions bout her schoolin or if she could cook or clean or had any special talents. The girl had no questions for him. This was a strange freedom for a young girl named Carrie Lee. She knew the situation when he asked her family could he marry their daughter; they just told her to get her things. She didn't need no extra time to wash and fold up and pack a car full of clothes.

She rolled up her one other shirt and one dress and carried it under her arm and was ready to go. He gave her daddy one hundred dollars and told him to come get one of his good smoked hams from the smoke house. Carrie Lee knew what her role was gon be. She knew he had no children. She was not pretty. Carrie Lee was thin and tired lookin cause there was very little food in her house to eat. Her skin was pale pink and her eyes were round and gray and empty lookin. Her hair was so light it looked almost white. She didn't have no boy friend or no dreams. When she got to Mr. Cecil's big house she was pleased to have her own room and could bathe whenever she wanted to. Mr. Cecil did not want her to look like she was bought so he did buy her some dresses and other women things she needed.

Carrie Lee was proud of her new things but never thanked him. She knew he would soon be knockin on her door, tellin her to undress, lay down and be stil. She did what he asked. Never complained bout any hurt or pain he caused on her. They never talked bout nothing. She was always in a hurry to wash off his musty smell and the wetness he left.

After he was gon, Carrie Lee enjoyed the peace she had to herself in her bedroom. He kept comin back at least twice a week til her period stopped. He knew she was pregnant.

After that he had no use for her. Wasn't no love, just baby makin. He provided for her and the child, even got one of the colored women to help with the first one and the four more that came after that.

She never named them, he did. Every single one of the boys had a name that started with an "H." The first one named Harvey, the next one named Harvis. The next one named Harris, the next one named Harbid and the last one named Herbin. So all of them boys had the same first letters alike in they name an H, and Hideaway for the last name.

She breastfeed each one of them boys, bathe them, rocked them to sleep, made sure they was safe but left the love part out. She gave that to Mr. Cecil to do. He spent time with his boys and talked to them. He rubbed their heads, patted them on the shoulder but wasn't no kissin or cuddlin, nowhere in sight.

Anyhow, once them boys were old enough to dress themselves, he gave Carrie Lee some money to move out and on. She didn't make no noise or do no cryin. She packed all her extra dresses and shirts in a good suitcase. She carried them and left with her sad gray eyes and no joy in her heart and never returned. Mr. Cecil told his boys she was gon and they would be fine, because they did not need her anymore. They were big enough to take care of themselves. Them boys looked real hard at their daddy but said nothing to him, just like their mother would do. He did let the colored women cook, clean and see after them boys, but that didn't take love, so he thought.

Anyway he took pride in makin sure he raised his boys the way his father raised him. After all, that was all he knew. Til they got out of high school the biggest learnin they got day in and day out was the work they did every day on that farm before and after school. Then they worked full time on that farm. Mr. Cecil wanted to make sure they would carry on his way. So whatever them five H named boys became they got from their momma and their daddy and no God they ever heard talk of.

Would you believe every single one of them boys looked like her? Not one of them boys showed no signs of Mr. Cecil. I take that back, they was tall like him but they was slim, with them gray eyes like her and that almost white hair. It was something to watch them boys grow up and have no joy on the inside like their mother. They didn't smile much and most of their talkin was carried on with their father. Them boys had decent clothes and shoes, plenty to eat, a bed to sleep in and could bathe anytime. They didn't want for nothing but as young boys the touch of true love was missin and they didn't even know.

Mr. Cecil had a patch of land that was deep with thick big trees close up on each other. He had the strong colored men that worked in his fields cut down only the ones he had roped off. They was the trees in the middle but the outside trees he left, the trees that was kissin each other.

He slowly took his time and had eight houses and a church built on the inside of them trees and a trail in front of them to go in and come out. Now we couldn't read his mind but as we worked we listened and watched and figured out on our own what Mr. Cecil was doin.

He wanted his own little community for his sons.

He wasn't a prayin man but he thought if he added a church, other white people would want to live there and bring some more bizness with them and maybe some more houses would be built.

When his youngest son reached eighteen and the oldest bein twenty three, he told each one of them boy's to "go find a young girl to marry and have some babies." He told them what kind to get and what town they could be found in.

His sons knew what was in store for them when their father died so they each went out and got them a young girl to marry in the new church. Now the ones they choose was just what they father asked them to get, poorly lookin and po.

Well, life went on with them boys and them young girls and them babies they was makin. They spent a lot of time drinkin whiskey, gamblin and sleepin with each other's young wives. I guess they was tryin to make up for all they lost.

Them boys didn't take care of them eight houses or spent no time worshipin in that little church either. They found no shame in what they was doin in them woods cause they thought wasn't nobody comin round lookin and wasn't nobody gon tell.

But their sin didn't stay no secret cause they daddy found out.

On most Sundays his sons and their families would have dinner with Mr. Cecil at his house. On one of them visits, two of them boys Harvie and Herbin sat round in the front yard laughin and talkin bout which wife they was gon make the next baby with and Mr. Cecil heard it.

He got real concerned, he didn't like what his sons was doin in his Hideaway town. He quietly got up from his seat in the yard and went in the house.

He came back and shot Harvie first in the leg and then shot Herbin in his leg to. He didn't kill them cause he needed them. They both walked with a cane for a while and made it seem like a joke with the folks in town. Mr. Cecil told his sons if they touched their brother's wife again or speak on who fathered which child he would disown them. Mr. Cecil didn't go to no jail or nothing. Everybody there told the Sheriff that the boys shot each other 'cause they was drunk and got crazy with a gun and that was that.

Mr. Cecil told his sons they did not turn bad til they moved. It didn't have nothing to do with how they was raised in his mind. He said "Them deep woods with all them trees and the houses built on that land were cursed and nothing good would come out of it".

Mr. Cecil had heard the stories bout the old woman bein buried under the dirt by the big tree. He had been told bout how the woman prayed as she walked at night in the woods among the big trees, but he held that tale inside his soul. He had been told as a child that when slaves prayed, they asked God to curse the land, so nothing would grow.

He ordered his sons and them wives, with them babies to move back home. He never talked bout or went to his town, Hideaway again.

He didn't think we had sense enough to know we knew bout the wisdom of the old woman and the strength of the people that came before us. We kept that secret to ourselves.

Now them eight houses and that church stayed empty and raggedy for a good while. Everything green and wild round them houses and that little church kept growin and spreadin and kissin and coverin up Hideaway like it was keepin it safe and a secret back up in them woods.

Mr. Cecil didn't give no thought to sellin them sinful small houses to other white people.

But as time passed he realized he could make money off them houses. Bein as sinful as that land was it was just right for colored people especially since slaves roamed there many years ago. But he kept that secret to himself. He wasn't concerned bout clearin no road or bringin Hideaway back to life. He said, "I'll let them decide how they want to live in Hideaway. It'll be up to them to clean it up."

He offered those shabby houses to anybody. He didn't do no checkin on your character or finances, he just took your money.

He had all the legal papers for you to sign sayin you was rentin it or buyin it, he didn't care. If you was late with your monthly payment he had somebody put you stuff outside the house. It wasn't no notice or grace period.

We knew Mr. Cecil did not care bout Hideaway or us.

Most of us who moved to Hideaway never looked at it as a place we was gon stay forever but it was a start to havin your own piece of something. Some of us that came didn't stay long cause money was sometime short dependin on who you worked for and where you worked. Mr. Cecil liked puttin people out cause there was always somebody who wanted to try ownin they own house. Those of us that held on didn't spend time braggin bout what we had, we spent time prayin, askin God for extra hours to work on whose ever farm, field, factory or house would pay us. We spent the other time fixin and doin what we could in our Hideaway.

We didn't give no time to what Mr. Cecil thought bout Hideaway, we were more concerned bout tryin to live better as best we could.

Before I get to anything else let me tell you bout our church.

4

Hideaway Peoples' Church

The church sat right in the middle of them eight houses. Four houses on one side of the church and four on the other side. We had to do a lot of redoin over cause by the time we got there, snakes, squirrels and all kinda creatures lived good. We washed and scrubbed a good while. We painted our little church white. There was two windows, one on each side of the front door and two on each side of the church. We got the paint from Mr. Cecil's shed but he didn't know it. Somebody worked slow and delicate like and painted pretty pictures of God and sheep and mountains from the Bible on them side windows, makin them look like they was stained glass. We had men who worked for Mr. Cecil but would sneak over when they could and get up on the roof of our church and patch up them holes so wouldn't no rain and air get in. The men was always workin on makin sure we had heat in the winter. We started with a hot stove and moved on up years later to a boiler. We took the front doors off our church. Somebody found a strong, heavy, thick, solid wood door that just set off our church some kinda good.

It's a mystery how God moves, and makes room for His work to be done for His good. When we all pitched in with sandin and glazin that wood til it shined it was beautiful in our church. It wasn't big and fine, as a matter of fact it was kinda small. A cross sat on the top of the roof that you could see wherever you sat on your porch.

One of our members knew how to take a thin paint brush and draw flowers and birds on our walls. We even had a septic tank put in so we could have us an inside restroom. We didn't have no air conditionin but we had some good fans.

Up on the wall behind the pulpit we had a cross that hung there strong and sturdy. In the pulpit there was just enough room for our pastor and 15 choir members to sit. We had an altar right in front of the pulpit, where a small table with a white lace scarf was placed to hold our big Bible. Anybody who needed to pray could stand or get on they knees right there before or after service was over. That pulpit, that little table and our pews was well made. We had some good carpenters in our church who made or fixed anything we needed. We truly had people with gifts we knew God gave them. We draped the podium with a red velvet scarf where the pastor stood to preach. We had a sister member who made two red cushions with gold trim and tassels on each end for the Pastor and guest to sit on. At Christmas time we used red covers on the back of the choir members chairs. When everybody wore something red, we all looked real pretty. Our trustees sat in the front pews on the left side of the church and the deacons sat on the front pews on the right side. One of them was always ready to assist with whatever the preacher needed.

You know the strange thing bout our little church, when folks from Hideaway and our county came together we always seemed to have enough room for everybody.

We had church every first, third, and fifth Sunday when one came in that month. When we had bad weather we had to preach to ourselves cause it was tough for anybody to get in or out of Hideaway. Our church was a place for worship but it was a meetin place as well. If you wanted to know who did what, when, and who with, you could find out up in the church. If you wanted to hear a good lie, and somebody get cussed out for it the church was the best place to be. If you needed to hear a joke that would make you laugh so hard your stomach hurt, or hear somebody give their testimony that would make you cry, we had a church that provided the quickest way for you to get it.

We couldn't pay no minister steady money, so most of the preachers we got came from the Bible school up the road. They was students learnin how to preach. In other words they was tryin out on us.

Some of them young preachers came with a sermon that could prick the spirit in a mighty way. It did not matter the size of our sin or pain, or anger, God was just movin from person to person, from heart to heart feedin each one as they needed it.

Them few preachers who didn't get lost, tryin to find Hideaway, was real serious bout spreadin the word of God. They didn't worry bout that red dust they was gon get on they car or they shoes. They were sent to bring the word to God's people. We knew they needed some gas money for comin so we took up a love offerin for them. We stil had to pay our light and water bill we got every month for the church. Mr. Cecil never said we had to pay anything for the church and we never received a tax bill or nothing. We was blessed and we knew it! We figured it out where if each one of our steady members gave two dollars apiece that would take care of that.

We had our good ushers who knew how to smile and be nice to get whatever we didn't get durin offerin time at the front door before members left after church was over.

Now how much them young preachers got depended on how the people took in the sermon and the movement of the Holy Spirit.

I think, this just my opinion, if you was hungry for the Word and you was truly fed by the messenger you would remember who God sent to feed you. So in other words that young preacher got more in his love offerin then somebody who had us flippin back and forth in the Bible an ain't said nothing that made sense.

When we served dinner after the service, we made sure they ate something before they left or we packed a good lunch for them to take. Somebody always had a pound of some kinda vegetables or smoked meat for them to take up the road.

We seldom got the same preacher twice in one month, so a few of us kept a list of the ones we wanted to preach for our special occasion programs. We got they phone number and address so we could reach them if we needed to.

To tell you how we did funerals and weddins would take another whole sit down talk, on another day. Dealin with church people on them two things can make you not like them.

Now we've had a couple of them wannabe-preachers who thought we was blind, couldn't hear and didn't have good sense.

We was always polite to them cause that's how God want us to be. But we scratched them off our list real fast cause they wasn't nothing but fools. Sometimes we got tired of them hittin and missin sermons.

In our little church there were so many times we had to remember that word thankful-ness; that kept us from complainin bout something we didn't have or criticizin somebody bout what they did or didn't do right or not at all. Them twin sins, complainin and criticizin coulda kept us all bitin and bickerin with each other. Now don't get me wrong, we was far from perfect. But when some of us saw that when we pulled together, trusted and thanked God the easier our heavy loads became, not only with each other in the church but in our homes, and our struggles with the outside world that didn't care nothing bout the people who lived in a place called Hideaway.

5

Them Eight Houses

There were four houses on one side of the church and four houses on the other side of the church. I told you bout that path you had to take to get up in Hideaway. It will bring you in but to get out you had to go round all them eight houses like you was ridin in a circle. You couldn't back out of Hideaway. You would hurt yourself, somebody else and your car.

Not all of my neighbors had the same idea bout fixin up and doin. Some of us had the same understandin when it came to bein neat and clean. But some of us was just nasty and we didn't have sense enough to know we was or was just lazy and didn't care.

Some folks had pretty flowers and real green grass. Some of us didn't have no flowers and no grass. Some of us had weeds growin every which-a-way, others didn't have weeds they had dirt. They didn't give the weeds and nothing else time to grow. Some of my neighbors had paint peelin off the side of their houses, and others had their house painted real nice.

One of my neighbors had a little garden in the back of their house. One of my neighbors had empty liquor bottles spread all over their front yard, another one had a rusted up car in their front yard that stayed there for a long while. One had parts and pieces of lawn mowers in his yard.

We never met or had no neighborhood club meetin or took up no dues to discuss any plans for makin Hideaway pretty to look at. We each came with our own how-we-was–gon-live plan. I'm sure some of us wanted better for Hideaway but when you peeked over and saw somebody's brokenness, anger, sorrow or loss, you didn't seem to notice what the outside of their house looked like.

It's a funny thing it didn't matter cause each one got the same amount of sunshine on a hot day or a cold one. When the wind blew we all could hear and look up and see those leaves on them trees swishin from side to side. We all could see the beauty of our big trees from one season to the next. When a thunder storm came we could feel the rumble and watch the lightnin. But when it came to measurin our darkest disappointment, our darkest sin, how much joy and pain that we carried on the inside of them houses depended on how each one of us lived our lives.

But before I start tellin you bout my neighbors I want you to know everybody got they own side to a story. Somebody coulda been standin right next to me, sittin on they own porch, eyein across the way, hearin the same thing like me, but that don't mean we both made sense of life in Hideaway the same way.

You might think you heard my neighbors talkin and tellin their own tale but it's just me talkin for them, puttin their story together the best way I know how. I ain't gon lie to you sometimes me and my neighbors would get together and claim to know exactly what our neighbors felt and said out they mouth, in their own house. So I'm gon tell you what we thought up in our own head they said. On one or two occasions I'm gon repeat what somebody told me out their own mouth cause they was right there in the middle of what was goin on. But please don't forget these people were my friends, at times my kin, and my lifeline. So I got to see them, and feel them up close and real personal. So with that bein said with some of my stories like your momma and daddy you only gon get a pinch cause some of my neighbors didn't stay no long time in Hideaway for me to tell you know more than that. For some you gon get the beginnin and the middle cause that's all I could piece together. With one or two, you may think you got the whole story but I'm gon leave that up to you to figure out.

Randell, my husband wasn't there no long time but I was there for a good while before leavin. Many of my neighbors was stil there when I left. I didn't get no addresses or phone numbers to keep up with them, so I can't give you no and they lived happily ever after report. I just prayed that each one did.

Now stay with me.

6

The Greens

Ernest Green had his own truck and towed anything to anywhere for anybody that would hire him. He got pretty good money especially when trees were cut down and the land needed to be cleared. He was a good mechanic too so he would fix cars on the side.

He had the sweetest wife. Her name was Tootie. She spent most of her time at home scratchin and readin. She had a bad rash that kept most of her body broke out, dry, and ashy. It took out most of her hair and affected her eye sight so bad she wore those real thick eye glasses.

They couldn't afford to go to no specialist so most of the medicines she used were homemade. She used some kinda ointment that had a strong smell to it. You didn't have to see her to know she was comin cause that odor came first. She was a very intelligent woman.

She went to school to be a teacher. So when any of us got some mail and we didn't quite get the meanin she was good at explainin things real easy like so you could get a good understandin. She taught Sunday school. Tootie always asked God for wisdom when she read and delivered the lesson in a manner that was pleasin in His sight.

Tootie would tell them stories out the Bible and put it to everyday life. We really enjoyed Tootie. She loved books and was always readin whenever you saw her. She read bout faraway places like Africa and China. She would talk to anybody who would listen bout whatever was goin on round us an in the world especially when it came to equal rights for black folks.

Tootie spoke as if she was a live reporter right there in the middle of the action. Ernest, that's his first name, would laugh and say, "One day 'um gon take my wife to them places." Durin church he sat close to his wife with his arm round her. He didn't pay no mind to her rashy skin or her little bit of hair. So you knew Tootie's ointment perfume didn't bother him none. When he smiled at her, you could see the love in his eyes. With that bein seen on Sundays we learned to breathe on that scent whenever we sat next to her in church. The love we had for Tootie was thicker than that salve she was wearin.

He had friends he went to school with that worked in a factory in New Jersey. They told him with the skills he had, gettin a job wouldn't be no problem. He couldn't wait to go. He asked the church to pray for him and his wife. Ernest told the church, "The Lord has blessed me to not only make more money but the job come with health benefits. Um gon see to it that my wife gets the best doctor and um gon save some money and take her to see them places she always talkin bout."

I bet he did just that cause he got a good heart and they knew how to pray and ask God for direction to guide them in their life. I just know they doin fine up there in New Jersey.

7

The Finches

In every neighborhood you had some folk you loved havin them as your neighbors. They looked out for you; they were dependable if you needed something. But then you had some neighbors you hoped and prayed they moved on someplace else but there was no place for them to go.

Well, let me tell you bout Frank and Ann Finches. They the ones that got the paint peelin off the house and aint got no grass. If you love the Lord at all we suppose to love our neighbor the way God loves us first. With the Finches it was real hard. The husband and the wife had five kids and every last one of them didn't have a stitch of home trainin. I mean none. If they were not stealin from you, they always wanted to see what you had up close. They was never proper and in order bout nothing. When they came to church they didn't know how to sit down and be stil. They was loud and they made noises and laughed at themselves.

One Sunday the whole family sat behind me in church. The children kicked the pew, popped gum and talked the whole service. If they wasn't talkin they was hittin one another. I couldn't hold it no longer. I turned round and said, "If yawl don't stop actin a fool, you better." Did not one of them parents say a thing to any of them children? I turned back round in my seat and asked the Lord to hold me back cause I was bout to raise hell right there in the church.

When we served food they was the first in line. They ate like they hadn't been fed. There was always enough for everybody if the Finches would have taken just one servin instead of two of everything. Wherever they sat, they always left a mess. There was food and crumbs all over their mouth, they hands and on the floor and the table. The Finches would wait round after everyone ate, and want the leftovers, but never wantin to help clean up.

Now it's a sayin that says "children live the way they learn." So if the children ain't got no sense you got to look at who raisin them.

Let me start with the parents. Frank Finches was a handsome smelly man. Ain't no sense in me lyin. I can't say it no nicer. He didn't bathe and he had bad breath. He always had the answer to your question even when you didn't get a chance to fully get your question out. He was always the first to volunteer to do something but you couldn't find him when it was time to do the work. His word was bout as short as his tight hair on his head.

He had a bad habit of pickin up stuff lookin it over but somehow it didn't get back where it was at first. If it did it was broke or missin a part. He cut grass for a livin so he was always repairin some kinda tool in his front yard which did not have a blade of grass no-where growin.

Now his wife was bout five feet and weighed maybe a hundred pounds. She was a little bitty thing with a whole lotta mouth. She talked real loud and would put her hands on her hips when she really thought everybody was listenin. She wore heels all the time but would always complain that her feet hurt.

She loved to lie just like her husband. They had to sit down and write down what big story they was gon tell us. She thought people really believed she owned a beach house, but come to find out it was a shack that belonged to her daddy. She worked in town in the dime store as the stock clerk. She always greeted you with a smile and a lively conversation. She knew where everything in the store was located and was excited to tell you bout any sale they was havin.

You know it's an amazin thing them Finches never found no fault in how they lived their life. They had no problem in comin to church or any other function we had late and loud. They would cuss you out if they thought anything was given out and they were not included. They was in church every Sunday we had church. She had them kids participatin in any program we had even though they caused confusion. They loved each other and God loved them too.

Some members grew in their faith and came to understand and decided one-by-one the battle was not gon be theirs to take on. So we had to pray and try and remind ourselves every time we saw them comin as hard as it was not to judge but to love them anyhow! I wonder how them Finches doin?

Let me move on.

8

The Morrises

Sandra and John Morris lived in the last house on the right side of the church. They're the ones that had liquor bottles all over their front yard and didn't care who saw them.

Sandra was a strange lady but the men would say she's a woman any man would love to have. She was real shapely and could strut in such a way that made all the right things on her body jiggle. She had burnt sandy colored skin with short light brown hair she kept wrapped in a scarf. Sandra had green eyes with a wide pudgy nose with wide lips to match. She wore high heel shoes all the time which made her look like a giant over people cause she was already very tall. She had big pretty legs that she showed off well with her loud colored dresses that tugged tight on her body. Sandra wore enough jewelry to give all the women in the church a piece to wear.

She was home much of the day but she stayed real busy durin the evenin hours. She kept a full house, of men friends who lived on the outside of Hideaway. She was married to an old man. He worked on the railroad at night. It was hard to believe he didn't know what was goin on in his house night after night. When you been livin with a woman or a man long enough you can sense things.

But he never tended to sensin those kinda feelins at all. Sandra made her money and them men knew whatever bizness they had with Sandra was strictly between them and her. None of her men folk ever said nothing to her husband out-the-way cause he carried a knife, and if you got in his face he would cutcha.

He didn't bother nobody, he only spoke if you spoke to him. He walked with his head down most of the time. He was a very tall, slim, man. What was interestin is that Mr. and Mrs. Morris looked more like father and daughter then husband and wife. He had the same colored hair, eyes and skin color. He even had a pudgy nose like hers.

But when they came to church both well-dressed once in a blue moon they came as husband

and wife. Nobody said a word, we just thought things in our heads. If you studied them long enough you could tell they was related. But we all had to be careful bout diggin in other folks' bizness cause we all had some secrets and sins locked away in Hideaway.

Time went on and one day, Mr. Morris was found dead in the woods. He had gon huntin and died. Somehow or another he slipped and fell. His knife that he always carried ended up deep in his stomach. Wasn't no investigation or nothing cause he was by himself and wasn't no white sheriff gon ask no questions bout our life or death.

Some said Sandra killed him. She could get some of her men folk to do whatever she needed help with. That came from people pokin round always believin the notion that Mr. Morris was her father and not her husband. They said she got tired of the kinda love Mr. Morris wanted from her. The small bits and tangled up pieces you heard made you sick. I mean stories like, Mr. Morris killed her mother and raised her and trained her to do and be what he wanted her to be. Another story was, her father caught his wife with another man. Mr. Morris was real jealous of his wife and hated her for what she did. So he took his daughter as his own, out of spite. But those are tales that had dark unseen bitter roots growin in Hideaway that only Sandra could tell.

Now I told you we would have to discuss how we do funerals at another sitdown but I got to tell you this. Sandra met us at the church and informed the members of the funeral arrangements.

"Um gon have the wake and the funeral in my house cause his spirit won't rest in the church."

Now we could've sat round an asked her, what she meant bout his spirit not restin in the church. But we didn't say not-one-word, we just listened.

Sometime, it's not important that we church people know all the details of some one's pain or sufferin to decide if we gon reach out to them in their time of need. When God said lean not on your own understandin. I think that's what he meant. That was not the time to figure out Sandra. We was suppose to help her and show love as best we could and pray for her.

The women stayed at the church to decide on who was gon cook what. The men walked Sandra back to her house and found Mr. Morris dressed in his Sunday suit layin on the bed with his arms folded just like he was in a casket.

She stood next to the bed and said, "I got some of his blood in a jar already in the ground so he can visit anytime"

When she said that, the men didn't ask Sandra any questions bout Mr. Morris's death. We all had heard stories bout blood in jars and how some of them men who came to her house didn't leave with all they common sense. So we went on with the funeral as she directed. She wanted everybody round that bed at sunset. The men brought chairs for a few of us to sit down but we weren't there long.

We didn't have a preacher. Sandra was wearin a green gown near bout the color of a lime. She had on jewelry to match that we couldn't help hear cause it was jigglin the whole time she was sprinklin good whiskey over his body and thankin the Lord for her father and her husband. Everybody in that room heard what she said and froze like death. But we said nothing.

When the service was over, Sandra said, "My husband gon be buried in them woods where they found his body."

Deacon Pearl said, "Sis Morris, you don't have to bury Brother Morris in them woods. It's hard to tote a body with all them trees."

"I got some men folk to dig the grave for me. It's already done," Sandra said with a don't-tell-me-what-to-do voice.

Deacon Pearl kept talkin. "You know we got a little cemetery behind the church, we got enough room to bury Brother Morris. You don't need any money. The men from the church can make you a casket."

Mrs. Morris answered quick. "No thank you. I want his body wrapped in the covers he layin on and I want him in them woods."

Her men friends did just as she asked and the men folk from the church pitched in.

Now some of that pitchin in was just so somebody from the church could see where Brother Morris was buried. Deacon Pearl went and came back and told us Sandra was dancin round bare footed sippin on that good whiskey. When she got tired she told the men to cover her husband with the dirt.

Once Mr. Morris's grave was covered she looked at them and said, "Thank you all for your help."

We heard Sandra strutted out them woods with her head held high, jigglin her jewelry and her body at the same time with a couple of her men folks trailin behind her. When she got back to her house some of our members took food to her and left. She thanked them and shut the door. Later that night it was normal we could hear them, as usual, she had a house full of men friends. I told you she was strange. Ain't no tellin all Sandra been through; people like that you got to know what you doin when you tryin to pray with them up close. We knew what we heard her say out her mouth bout her husband and father but she knew no one was gon ask what she meant by that. None of us could help her fix it. We really thought the best we could do was to pray for her at a distance and trust that God would comfort, heal and free Sandra from all, deep hurt, deep harm and deep darkness.

I wonder where that child at.

9

Ella Mae

Remember me tellin you we had folks who lived in Hideaway and we was glad they left. Well I'm gon tell you bout one of my neighbors. An elderly couple, Otis and Clara Cooper. That was one of the first couples to move to Hideaway. They had worked for Mr. Hideaway for years as pickers and Clara washed and ironed for them for a long time. When they got up in age they announced to the church their granddaughter was comin to live with them.

Now aint no body crazy. If you was young and came from a place where black folks could make a livin but you left to live with somebody in Hideaway it meant one of two things, either you was runnin from something or you had nowhere else to go.

The Coopers had the house with the raggedy car in the front yard I was tellin you bout. That car killed their nice little yard the moment their granddaughter, Ella Mae Beasley drove all the way from Detroit Michigan to Hideaway.

Now she got some ways on her that will give you a headache tryin to figure her out. She would lie, steal and hurt people.

One of her favorite sayins was "um fixin to."

She was always tellin us neighbors she was fixin to get her car fixed but it didn't get fixed. It sat and rusted.

She was always fixin to get a job real soon but never got round to it.

Ella Mae kept herself busy workin on the bereavement committee in our church. They helped members who lost love ones anyway they could. They took food to them, helped them with the funeral arrangements, cleaned they house or just sat and held they hand to comfort them. Ella Mae never cooked nothing, helped with the funeral plans but she was fixin to. Her talent was her sweet charm. She could rub up on you and put you under a spell if you wasn't payin attention especially the men folk. They was busy lookin at her breast cause they was the biggest things on her and she always had them showin.

She would go to their house and leave with an arm full of clothes, a pocket full of jewelry and another sack of whatever else she thought the dead didn't need no more. She always told her grandmamma and anybody who asked, "They was give-a-ways from the family." So the bereaved people ended up bein a real comfort to her.

Well, one Sunday Ms. Ella Mae had the nerve to wear one of them give-a-way outfits and the trimmins to go with it to church. She had on the suit, wore the hat, and carried the gloves in her hand and the purse on her arm. She wore the suit well; it was huggin in all the right places. A whole lotta eyes were on her. She looked good but she got there late and had the nerve to squeeze in and sit on the second row in the front.

Ella Mae had no idea that the woman sittin in the row behind her paid no attention to how good she looked but kept lookin at that suit she was wearin and all the trimmin to go with it. She sat payin no attention to the sermon but lookin and thinkin bout that suit. She realized she hadn't touched her mother's clothes since the funeral. So she had to think back how Ella Mae got a hold of her momma's things out of her momma's closet without her knowin.

She remembered Ella Mae comin to her house, spendin a lot of time pattin on her father's knee and rubbin on his back. She didn't want to leave her father alone but she had to get her hair done for the funeral so she thought she was leavin her daddy in good hands. When she returned home her father was sleep and Ella Mae was gon. When that child figured out how she walked out with her momma's things she got to jumpin and shoutin. At first everybody in church thought the daughter was caught up in the spirit but when she leaped over the pew and undressed Ella Mae, that's when some of the members of the church realized it wasn't the Holy Ghost.

The trustee board held an emergency meetin when they got a hold of what Ella Mae was doin. The Chairmen paid her grandparents a visit; they felt it would be a good idea if Ella Mae was a member of another church. Her grandparents knew everybody in Hideaway and that little town knew or would know bout Ella Mae's ways. So Ella Mae said "don't worry 'bout me I'm gon be alright." She caught a ride to the next town with one of them visitin preachers and left that rusted car in that yard.

Ain't that something. We had heard she got a job up there. She did come back from time to time and visit her grandparents. One night was real excitin. She brought a guitar player to Hideaway. We had a concert right there on her grandparent's porch. He sang some down home blues we drank some down-home whiskey and got tow up. We enjoyed it but we was glad when he and she quietly left. Soon after that we heard she got married but it wasn't Mr. Guitar man.

Now she knew her sins were stil fresh in the minds of her old church family, so she came home to show off her new ring and a husband to make folks think she had changed her ways. The first time Ella Mae brought him home to meet her Hideaway family he made quite an impression. His name was Clarence and his car was not rusty. He paid somebody to move Ella Mae's old car.

He was a dark-skinned man with pretty white teeth who wore tinted glasses so you never really saw his eyes. He was a quiet man who spoke and laughed in a slow deep voice. He walked round durin the day with his hair tied-up so he wouldn't mess up his process. He had nice waves but we only saw them on Sunday when they came to church. You could tell he liked nice things cause he wore them suits that laid just right without a wrinkle anywhere and a shiny ring on his pinky finger.

Clarence walked like a cool dude or a pimp as we old folks would say.

Ella Mae bragged to us after church bout the job she was fixin to get sellin vacuum cleaners. Her grandparents were happy but Clarence seemed to set his self apart not sayin a word. He got a car for her and her vacuum kit. She went from one county to another sellin to people in beauty shops, the taverns and the restaurants. Ella Mae always got paid every Friday though.

One time she got robbed so Clarence bought her a little bitty gun. She didn't get robbed no more with that vacuum cleaner. But one night late we had some strangers to ride up in Hideaway lookin for Ella Mae. They didn't have a problem knockin on our doors askin had we seen her.

They left a message with us to tell her they was waitin on their vacuum cleaner money. We never really knew what Ella Mae was doin up there but her mess got all the way to Hideaway. Ella Mae always had money on her. Soon after that she quit the vacuum cleaner bizness and was back in Hideaway.

Ella Mae was with her grandparents til they died. The house was hers now and everything in it. She often complained to us that Clarence tried to get her to sell it but she told us she told him he could leave cause she was gon be alright, she didn't need him. Ella Mae had a money plan but it did not include him. We knew Clarence was angry cause he hit her in the face. She did not change her mind or leave with him. Her face was blue and black for a long time and her left eye never look the same.

She went to work for a bookie. She made pretty good money. I know cause I hit a couple times myself. People didn't try to rob her cause they knew she had a chip on her shoulder, carried a small gun and she would not hesitate to use it.

Ella Mae stil had her slickish ways bout her. She thought it was alright to take a little bit extra of her new boss's money and buy some things she needed. She got hit in the face again but this time she laid there in the front yard where her rusty car use to be and died.

10

The Reverend
Theodore Lucas Showall

Before I tell you bout my other neighbors I gotta stop right here. You got to hear bout this one man and his wife who broke in our church and said the Lord sent him and his wife. I wouldn't tell you one word of a lie!

Somebody, I forget who it was—said they saw a light on in the church late one night. They went to the church and knocked on the door but nobody answered and the door was locked.

They knew Sister Hazewood our trustee member had a key, but decided not to bother her.

I know who it was now, it was Brother Miller.

He probably was drinkin and didn't want Sister Hazewood to be askin him no questions bout that whiskey smell on his breath, but anyhow let me go on with what happen.

The next day he didn't need to get no key, the church was wide open.

Everybody heard and saw for themselves we had us a preacher. He was singin and preachin and havin church with himself and his wife.

People came on in and sat down real calm like. He kept on preachin and singin and havin church. He talked real strong. You didn't have to wrinkle up your face to understand his words. They soaked right on down to your soul like soft butter on hot toast.

After his sermon, he walked up close and looked at each person straight in their eyes. It was a little spooky. He didn't have no smile on his face.

He was a big man with a big wife.

She sat on the front pew stuck in a place somewhere. Her hands in her lap and her head held stiff-out-straight. She wasn't lookin and seein none of her husband's soon-to-be flock. But we'll get back to her later.

Let me finish tellin you bout our new pastor.

He was a good six feet and bout six more inches added on to that. He had smooth baby soft midnight black skin and eyes that were not brown like most black folk.

They was a reddish color that would make anybody sit up straight and listen to whatever he had to say cause he was scary lookin. He had a lot of gray hair in his head which was pasted down with grease.

When he walked across the floor I couldn't help but notice his shoes, they squeaked, they were worn clean out. They looked as though they got wet from walkin in high water for a long time and he dry um out on somebody's stove.

His navy blue jacket and suit pants didn't have a press nowhere. They looked as if they had been soaked in hot water cause his britches was fittin up round his ankles and the hem of his jacket was high up on his back.

He had on a gravy-stained white shirt with safety pins instead of buttons to hold it together.

"I am The Reverend Theodore Lucus Showall The Third from Whuppa City Mississippi. The Lord my God sent me here to pastor His people. He told me not to worry bout how I would be paid."

Now them words alone stung everybody for a hot minute cause number one we ain't got no money and we ain't asked God for him!

He continued on, "God told me not to worry bout how I was gon take care of my wife, He just told me to go."

When the members heard that, some of us got to lookin round at each other cause the Lord didn't tell him to go break in the church.

I had never seen anything like it. He kept talkin, I think he knew most of us wasn't feelin him, you know what I'm sayin.

"God sent me here to do a mighty work. And I'm gon do what thus says the Lord right here at Hideaway People's Church."

Sister Miles, another member moved closer to the new Hideaway People's Church wannabe preacher. She went to open her mouth when the Reverend moved right into a prayer.

"Lord I thank you for bringin me and my wife to this place. I thank you for this flock and for choosin me as their shepherd. I ask Lord that you bring your flock and your shepherd together as one. I ask that you sweeten the spirit of your people to receive this humble preacher and his wife, that they will be a generous people to their new pastor and first lady of the church.

Lord send down an angel tonight, one who will provide us a place to rest our tired bodies so we can rise and do great works. I pray oh God that through your love we will grow and be prosperous. I pray oh God that you receive our prayer requests and we claim that all we ask shall be given in the name of Jesus, amen and amen."

After the prayer Sister Miles gently escorted the Reverend and the first lady to our little church office. "Bless you my angel, bless you." That's what the Reverend said. I wouldn't tell you one word of a lie!

Now I got to stop right here, remember when I told you his wife sat the whole time stuck stil. It was like that woman was hidin deep behind one of those big trees all by herself.

She was a big woman but she wasn't fat. She was big boned all over but firm. She showed no joy in her face so you couldn't tell if there was any goodness on the inside.

But on the outside she reminded me of a queen. She wore her hair back in a tight bun high on her head. No hair in her face, just the beauty of perfect skin that had no wrinkles or sags.

With her high cheek bones, and deep set almond shaped eyes she seemed mysterious, the kind that would trap a man.

Her full shapely lips were made like the ones you see women who wear that wild red lipstick but hers were thinly glazed with a hint of pink showin through. Her outfit was way different from his. From her head to her toes looked like somebody had or got some money from some where. She wore a purple dress that clung neatly over her body to just below her knees.

She had on one of them knitted shawls draped round her shoulders filled with pink and lavender butterflies She wore purple suede pumps, and carried a purple purse and gloves to match. Her Bible rested on her lap with her hands restin on top like that sittin arrangement was a natural thing for her to do. The strange thing was her shoes had a good heel on them and wasn't nothing on her stained or hand washed in hot water like his was.

Miss First Lady didn't show us she felt the way he did.

She was in a place all by herself and if you tried to call out to her in any form or fashion she wouldn't answer. I guess that was her secret covered up deep in the woods just like Hideaway.

Sister Miles offered them some cold water and asked them if they needed to use the restroom.

The Reverend commanded, "Take us where we can rest; we are a bit tired and I need to prepare for my sermon."

Now you know he was bout crazy as a roach.

Sister Miles told him gently to wait; she would be back in a minute. She went and told the men folk who was meetin in the church what he said.

Now they had already decided he wasn't in his right mind. His outfit to start with was a dead give-away. They couldn't figure out the wife but whatever was goin on with them was not bout the Lord!

Brother Baylor and your daddy, Brother Edwards, our two strong members told Sister Miles they was gon take care of it. Now the two of them were good men but they knew mess when they saw it.

And when you been round mess and did some messy things you know what a hustler looks like and we had one and his wife in Hideaway.

Anyway they went in and had a talk with Reverend and his misses. They didn't stay too long. Reverend Showall came out loud sayin we was all gon burn in hell and God would not forgive us for treatin a true man of God the way we did.

The First Lady was stil stiff and stuck somewhere.

Your daddy got close up on The Big Reverend and talked real low. The next thing we knew him and Brother Baylor escorted them out of the church.

The Reverend and the wife didn't have no car so somebody mustta dropped them off on purpose.

Brother Edwards was the one who decided to take them to the bus station in the next town. He told Brother Baylor to hold them and their two raggedy suitcases in the front of the church til he got back.

He went home and came back with his pistol and that big faced dog of his sittin up front on the passenger side with his big tongue hangin out the window.

That dog could bite a hole out your hind part, you hear me!

When Reverend Stowall saw the dog with Brother Edwards we saw a different side to the preacher. He started usin four-letter words and called us a bunch of back woods ignorant so-and-sos.

Brother Edwards made sure the Reverend saw his gun. He carried they luggage and put it in his trunk. He came round to the driver's side and said, "You and your wife can sit in the back or start walkin." I wouldn't tell-you-a-word-of-a-lie!

Mrs. First Lady, "stiff and stuck," finally had something to say. "I'm not walkin" she spat out, openin the car door for herself to sit in the back seat.

Rev. Theodore Stowall walked round to the other back door sat down and slammed it. They didn't say nothing to each other.

Brother Edwards looked back at both of them the way you would two kids you dare to-cut-the-fool, and warned them, "If na-ray-one of-yawl move, touch my dog, or me, I'm gon shoot somebody" and drove off.

Brother Edwards came back late that afternoon and went straight home. He didn't give us a let-me–tell-you-what-happened report and nobody went to his house and tried to get one cause everybody knew not to ask.

It wasn't no long time after that we heard that the Reverend ran into some more trouble.

He broke into the wrong somebody's house while they was gon and started treatin it like it was his own, eatin they food and bathin and carryin on!

When the owner got home he didn't want to hear Reverend Showall's sermon. He didn't call no sheriff, he just got to whippin up on him real bad and was askin God to give him strength the whole time.

The interestin part was when we heard some how or another Stiff and Stuck wasn't no where round. She got away with her raggedy suitcase, stil wearin her nice purle outfit.

I wouldn't tell you-one word of a lie!

You know for yourself when somebody claim to be your new preacher, breakin in the church, lookin like a hobo don't sound like God's doin. When he acted like he just came down off the mountain to save the lost people and a wife who is stuck somewhere else don't sound like God's doin. It looked more like the devil was movin round tryin to stir up some mess in Hideaway. I wouldn't tell you one word of a lie!

11

Deacon Pearl

Deacon Theodore James Pearl Jr. and his wife Laylean lived in the first house on the left side of the church with his parents. When his parents got up in age he took over where they left off, everything was neat and nice. That grass kept a haircut. He would not allow weeds to grow long enough to think they was at home. Paint stains was forever curled up under his nails cause he wouldn't let no faded paint or rust show nowhere.

Deacon Pearl worked the same way on the inside of the house. The furniture was built up real good so he made sure dust never slept on it. When you walked in the front door, shiny wooden floors looked at you as if to say, "Take your shoes off if you gon walk on me." It didn't take you long to look round and see he was an educated man, all them degrees and awards hangin and sittin round everywhere.

But Deacon Pearl never carried on bout his family's neat and nice inside and outside house or his education. If you went to visit and mentioned how good everything looked he'd smile and say, "Thank you, I'm blessed," then quickly offer you something to drink and whatever he was cookin or cooked.

Now I didn't say too much bout his wife in the beginnin cause Laylean left him and went back home to her own family. But I'm gon get to all that later. Right now let me finish givin you the background on Deacon Pearl and his momma and daddy.

His parents got there round the same time me and Randell did. They was both teachers. They taught in the only grammar school we had for colored children. They was two hard workin people. They had their one and only child Theodore James Pearl. They both called him TJ proudly, like they knew he was gon mount to somebody special. And he did!

He was the smartest non good lookin child in the whole school. He could out read, write and think most of the children beyond his years. He didn't let his cross-eyes under those glasses of his or skinny frail body get in the way of his joy. He was never a stingy child or grew up thinkin he was better. Theodore never wanted to be first or be seen. He just wanted to be apart, just a humble, down to earth person. His good ways called him out.

Theodore grew up and graduated number one in high school.

With all that book sense and church learnin he didn't spend much time playin in the yard with the other kids. But he did ask a quiet, pretty, dark chocolate girl to his senior graduation dance. That girl was Laylean Tiggs. Now Theodore's parents couldn't understand why he wanted to be with that child, knowin she wasn't nothing like him.

He met her in Sunday school when they both was bout eleven or twelve years old. They got baptized at the same time. But everybody was excited over the savin of two souls, wasn't no signs they was gon ever be married.

So when that child said yes she would go to the dance with Theodore, his parents had to go long with it. Them Pearls could not believe how beautiful Laylean looked.

Just cause her family made corn liquor for a livin didn't mean they didn't have class. I'm not gon lie to you. Laylean made their son handsome. With Theodore in his black fancy suit held her elbow as she strutted like a queen in her green sequined gown with her hair swirled up high on her head. That boy grinned all over his self. Them Tiggs and them Pearls were proud of their children that night. It had nothing to do with who was raised how, it was bout lovin your child and knowin it was a very special time in their lives.

The Pearls were not worried; after all, Theodore got an eye and mind full his entire life bout gettin an education. For him learnin was like livin, he wore it every day. His parents wanted great things for him.

They thought once Theodore went off to college he would do well, and meet the right kinda girl to fall in love with and marry. That boy went on to one of them black colleges somewhere but came home every summer. Laylean didn't come to church often but always seem to know when that boy was home.

She put a spell on him that stayed the whole time he was in school.

Now, let me tell you what was goin on with Laylean while he was gettin educated. I slipped and told you already her daddy and momma made corn liquor for a livin, which was dangerous for us folks. But they knew how to make money and deal with the police too. Now, you couldn't be scared to do that. So, they was bizness people.

The Tiggs also ran a juke joint. We could dance, buy a fish sandwich, drink corn liquor or a cold soda every Friday and Saturday night. You could buy a shot, a pint or a gallon jug. If you drank too fast or too much that corn could make you feel like the back of your head was on fire. I've seen for myself it can make you lose your mine and act a pure fool and live to regret it. Well, while all that was goin on Laylean got an eye and mind full. For her, whiskey was like livin, she wore it every day.

Now her parents made sure LayLean never wanted for anything. When she was in school she wore nice dresses and good shoes and that didn't change after high school. She got paid every week for helpin to run the family bizness. When she took a delivery with her father she got paid extra. Her job was to double count just in case her daddy got to talkin to somebody and forgot what he was doin. Laylean knew where her parents kept their guns and was taught how to use them if anybody tried to rob them or get foolish. For graduation, her father bought her a small gun, one she could carry in her pocket if she needed it. She was a smart girl and loyal to her parents. But a plan of goin to college wasn't talked bout in her house. The Tiggs wanted great things for Laylean and their corn liquor bizness could make that happen.

Now stay with me.

We got to get back to Theodore. He kept his mind on his studyin and Laylean. When his schoolin was over that boy came home with two degrees. Did you hear what I said? He went lookin for her with a ring.

His momma tried to tell him.

"You were not raised that way. That girl lived with whiskey all her life. Her family has been in the whiskey bizness for years. What makes you think she don't mind the smell or the taste. God's got something better for you."

His father said nothing but Theodore could see the hurt in his father eyes. He thought his momma and daddy believed they was better than the Tiggs. But he was set on bein with that girl. He found her fryin fish in the Juke joint. She was so glad to see him. She was just as pretty as she could be.

I told you he wasn't known for his looks but when that boy smiled he was just as handsome as he could be. Well, he married that girl. They got married in our church. He taught biology and chemistry in a high school not too far from Hideaway while Laylean continued to work in the family bizness. Theodore brought his bride home to live with his momma and daddy til they could move away. His parents were kind to Laylean. She knew how they felt but saw for herself that they loved their son and she was a part of him. It was never a discussion bout her makin no change in her profession. She would tell you, "Um in the whiskey bizness."

Theodore's momma got sick. She would come out of one illness and go right into another. First it was pneumonia, and then it was her kidneys. Some said his momma worried herself to death over that marriage.

Laylean was right there with Theodore and his father takin care of his momma. His momma got to see the kind side to her daughter- in- law. She knew that girl loved her son. But that wasn't enough. So she had to keep that secret way down deep in them woods.

Do you know his momma died? You ain't heard the worst part. Theodore's father started drinkin after that. Now we never smelled no liquor breath on him while he was on duty. He was in charge of our usher board. Any Sunday mornin we had church, Brother Pearl Sr. would help with devotion if somebody was late. He would greet and guide you to a seat and offer you a fan. Brother Pearl would even give you change for a five if you needed it and always sat on that back pew by the door to greet the late comers.

Let me tell you how we found out bout his drinkin. We spotted him, a couple of us members was buyin a pint from the Juke Joint. When you got the exact amount for your whiskey, it don't take long for you to slip in and out. But we knew that was him. Theodore knew what his daddy was doin but didn't say not a word and Laylean didn't say nothing either. Some of us knew what it felt like to be a private drunk. I know bout that myself.

I'll tell you bout me later. But a few of us that drank talked after church one Sunday and planted our own story how Pearl Sr. would go home and go straight to his room and drink by himself. Theodore and Laylean knew when he was drunk cause he probably was in his room cryin out to the Lord. When you dealin with your demons everyday it is a fight. It is the deep call we have to make to God to truly win the battle. But the recovery date depends on our will to lean on God. We truly believe on one of those drunken Sundays his father had the courage to tell his son how he really felt. We could see Theodore knockin on his father's bedroom door. His father cracked the door, but wouldn't let him in and waited for his son to speak. Theodore askin, "Why are you doin this to yourself?"

We could just hear his father with his whiskey breath "Son, I hope you will never know what a bitter love feels like. For your mother to love you so deeply and be so deeply angry with you at the same time, killed her. She allowed your decisions to eat away at her life and miss out on what God had for our life together as husband and wife. And I watched and said nothing and now she's gon and now I an tryin so hard not to hate you."

His father probably closed his door. Theodore knew exactly what his father meant. He knew he had terribly disappointed his momma and his daddy. With all that education he did not leave Hideaway and go do great things and to top it all off, he didn't marry the right kinda woman. Theodore knew that secret had to stay hid in them woods.

We were not surprised when one of those cold winter Sunday evenins Pearl Sr. was found by himself in his room lyin across the bed dead with his jar in his hand. He had a stroke. Theodore was not home at the time and Laylean was visitin her family. Theodore was all to pieces when he found him.

After his father's funeral, Theodore and Laylean decided to stay right there in that house in Hideaway and move forward. Some of us felt as quiet as Laylean was and with both of Theodore's parents dead she would not have to worry bout how they felt bout her anymore. She could show her tail.

But we kept quiet and watched and had the nerve to prophesize on what we thought their future was gon be like.

Every mornin they left together. She packed him a lunch and her one too. He dropped her off at her parents' house to make good whisky and he went to teach children. He picked her up every evenin and they went on home.

Theodore didn't pay much mine to his wife's whiskey breath every evenin when he picked her up or the slight scent of a cigarette. Laylean's sippin and samplin whiskey was not a thought he carried round. Their drop off and pick up arrangement went on for a good while.

But Laylean's parents were gettin older and needed her to work longer hours on the weekends. She knew one day she was gon have to take over the family bizness. Her and Theodore talked bout it and agreed it would be OK for awhile til they decided to work on a family. Theodore didn't have no problem with comin home and doin for himself cause his parents taught him well. Plus he was always doin things in the church most nights. So he would drop her off and her father or who-ever would take her home. Now that worked good for a while. But Laylean came home actin like she had more than a sip of whiskey. But Theodore didn't say nothing. Now that worked for another while til she came home drunk one Friday night.

She wasn't no drunk that got the fightin or cussin. She'd seen enough of that to know you can't drink up all the liquor and sell it too. Her father had to bring her in the house. She did not look Theodore in the face. Laylean slept in her clothes. Theodore watched and said nothing.

Now, let me say this to you. We loved Deacon Pearl and he knew we did. He also knew that we knew what was goin on with him and Laylean. But he didn't ask nobody to pray for him. We loved that child like he was our own so we kept havin our own prayer meetin and story tellin time bout what we thought was goin on between them two in their house but we didn't, say one word. We just kept quiet and kept spyin.

Anyway he sat in the chair in the bedroom and looked outside at the clear moon thinkin bout his parents and what he was told bout his wife.

Saturday mornin he decided he needed to talk to Laylean. He fixed breakfast and made coffee. She sat at the table in her drunk clothes. He served her breakfast. He learned that from his momma.

She ate and he talked.

"Laylean I love you and I knew when I married you what your parents did for a livin but if you're workin for them is causin you to come home drunk I will take care of you so you do not have to go back."

Laylean put her coffee cup down and said "Theodore I've been makin, sippin and sellin whiskey all my life. At times I may sip too much but I come home to you. That's all it was."

"We will see if that is all it will be Laylean," he said back.

He gently kissed her on the forehead and said, "I will be at the church; let me know when you are ready for me to take you to your parents."

It was not too much later before Laylean was comin home drunk right often. He stopped cookin breakfast cause she needed more time to sleep it off.

Finally it got to the point that it did not matter if it was a Friday or a Tuesday Laylean was drunk all the time. Most times Theodore had to take her clothes off and put her to bed.

That next mornin Theodore begged Laylean not to go back, he would take care of her.

Let me say one more thing. Deacon Pearl got up with the power to work and do for others every day with deep sorrow in his spirit. He didn't stop to hug his sadness with his momma or his daddy and with all he went through with his wife. He had the strength to run with patience, leanin on God, ain't that something!

Now, let me get back to Laylean. Laylean got to the point she wasn't comin home. But then another day passed and another so he decided he was goin to get his wife. Now we had heard and some of us saw her drunk as a fish. But we didn't offer her no prayer time, or ride home.

He found her sleep bent over a table. She had the same clothes on she wore when she left the house two days before. Now let me say this. Her momma and daddy never had a word to say bout they daughter. They taught her everything she lived. They never told Laylean not to marry that boy. They didn't know no better. If you drunk you drunk and you sleep it off til the next time.

Theodore softly picked his wife up not to disturb her from her sleep and placed her in the car. When Theodore got home he sweetly carried her in the house. He undressed Laylean and placed her in bed. He quietly smoothed the covers round her and got on his knees to pray. Tears flooded his face as he asked God to cleanse his wife of her whiskey soaked soul. The next day she called and reached out to him. Theodore went to her and held her close. Laylean cried and told Theodore she knew he would come for her. He rocked her in his arms and he cried askin God not to take is wife from him.

Laylean told Theodore after she had rested for a few days she was not goin back but she needed to let her parents know what her plans would be since they depended on her.

Theodore dropped her off like he use to and went on to work. It was three days before Laylean got home. Someone had dropped her off at the front door. He open the door to see her with a busted lip and a cut over her eye where she fell tryin to walk she was so drunk. She said "Why didn't you come for me"? Her clothes were torn and smelled of urine and vomit. Theodore gently took her in his arms and carried her to the bedroom. He undressed her and placed her in the warm tub. He bathed Laylean and sang to her. He cried to the Lord and asked God to shower down on Laylean. He asked God to give him strength to forgive his wife and remove the hatred that was buildin up inside of him. He dried his wife ever so softly and kissed her body. He rubbed her skin with lotion and covered her up with a gown.

He carried her to bed and sat next to her prayin for his wife as she slept. He thought bout his growin up, his schoolin and his parents. He thought bout what he coulda, shoulda been doin with his life.

He was stil sittin there when she woke up. They both looked deep and long into each other's eyes. They didn't touch or kiss just breathed slow longin to be close up on each other. Theodore got up from where he was sittin with his fist tight. "I'm sorry I did not come for you. I won't ever be comin for you so you don't have to be thinkin I will. I'm leavin for church and you need to leave." Now would you believe this was Sunday mornin when he said them things? He left for church.

Laylean went back to her whiskey filled life. She never did come back and he never did go get her. He never asked us to pray for her but that don't mean he didn't. We don't know what life was like for him when he went home. We would see Laylean whenever we wanted a good fish sandwich and what not. She never asked bout how Theodore was doin and we never gave him a report on her doins either. We never saw him with nobody after that. And we never heard talk of Laylean havin anybody special.

Now most people change up when they lived what he went through. He didn't. He was so smart. He went back to school. Can you believe that! That boy got a doctor degree. He got a job at one of them big companies doin research. He stayed in Hideaway and drove back and forth every day. But he kept workin in the church. He started travel all by his self, goin to far away places we dreamed of goin, we knew cause he would share with the church when he was gon be gon. Now, he was a true Deacon in every sense of the word. I mean a Christian from the inside out. He was there for you if you was sick, if you was dyin or dead. Deacon Pearl loved the Lord and didn't mind sayin so. He was up in the church in the winter time makin sure that little bit of heat we had was on and workin and the same thing with the fans in the summer. He had the keys to every door in the church and knew where everything was and knew where to look if you lost something. He never rushed us if we met longer then we was suppose to.

He would say, "I don't have any place to be."

12

Sister Basset

Sister Bassett's house stayed raggedy lookin for a good while til she met Smitty Reed. Now I can't tell you bout Smitty til I tell you what I know bout Sister June Basset. She was one who came to Hideaway with her baby girl JuneNet and no man. She was real stand off-ish. She never talked bout where she was from or her family. But if you stayed in Hideaway long enough someone would make it their bizness to find out bout you or tell a lie on you that somebody might believe and they go tell somebody else. So, we knew at some point the story on Sister Bassett was comin.

She was a pale, dough faced, light skinned women with real straight hair that didn't need no heat, no head rag and no grease to keep it straight. She didn't have no big lips or no wide nose. She was tall, slim with no fat on her. She had gray eyes and long light blondish brown hair that was always braided. We thought, she always walked as if something or someone was pressin her to get where she was goin.

She spoke if you spoke to her. It didn't matter how big your greetin was, hers was always the same, stale. There was never a smile, but a frown that sunk deep in the lines of her face that made her look sour and tired. It was as if she hated us knowin she was really one of us but not wantin to be a part of us.

We was round there thinkin on our own that where ever she came from, there was some trouble and she wanted to leave it where she left it. We never treated her bad, we just let her mistreat herself. You see it took a lot of strength to wear that kinda pain she carried every day.

She never knew some of us was always prayin for everybody in Hideaway includin her and her child. But one Sunday mornin, she came up in the church with her baby girl JuneNet. She sat quiet and to herself. Didn't none of us make no fuss over her or the baby. But we was smilin all inside though. She came back on another Sunday and then another Sunday. We could stil see signs of her hush-hush anger and that tired deep frown she wore. But you know what better place to be in for God to fix you and remove all that stuff we dress in and feel on the inside.

Before we left church our young visitin preacher had us get into groups of no more than four people. We didn't know what he was doin, but we did it. He asked us to pray out aloud for ourselves, our family and for the person on each side of us. We all just talked to God out loud at the same time. You know when you talkin to the Lord bout your own self you ain't listenin to nobody else's cry. But that particular Sunday we heard Sister Basset's cry out loud. I guess we were happy and noisy at the same time.

She shouted, "Lord my neighbors don't know me but I have seen and heard them gather and whisper bout my past road and the one I'm on now. God, let them know you planted me here with my child to live til you press me on somewhere else. But while I'm here please forgive me Lord. I have carried a heavy bag of hate for so long, please help me take it off my shoulder and let it go. Give me strength to raise my child and not allow my secrets to haunt her as they have haunted me."

We knew her prayer request was for God. It was never meant for us in that small group to put our heads together and come up with a how-to plan. Many of us knew bout deep love, deep sin and deep hate. We struggle with forgivin others. We all had secrets and mysteries in our lives that people would not understand. We knew our job was to pray that God's will, would be done for Sister Bassett and her baby girl JuneNet. But when she left after the prayer with her pressin-and-in-a-hurry-walkin self with her baby girl on her hip, we couldn't wait to have a gossip circle meetin. We knew that whenever we was secretly somewhere tryin to figure her out she wasn't no where to hear what we was sayin.

We got close and dug a little deeper in our circle of wisdom and came out sayin the same thing, "Sister Bassett wasn't anybody to mess with cause she could read people real good. She stayed in her place after that, didn't do no huggin when she saw you, door–to door visitin or askin to borrow a cup of sugar. We stil didn't know much bout her, or called her by her first name, June. But when you just wait, God has a way of bringin folks out into the light, for people to see who they are when He gets ready.

It happened right outside the church.

Remember me tellin you bout them Finches. Well one of them bad tail kids was runnin and fell on some ice. He got a big cut up side his head and didn't get up.

For a minute most of us folks didn't pay that child no mine. The mommy and daddy was all to pieces but Sister Bassett heard all that noise and came out to see what was goin on, just as calm. She gave her baby girl to one of the sisters to hold and she went to work. She turned that child over and was checkin to see if he was breathin like a doctor person would do. Then she asked somebody to bring her some cold, clean snow. She took that cold snow and patted his forehead with it. He woke up and she spoke real soft like to him. She told his parents he needed some stitches and she could do it.

She gently helped that boy up and took him to her house. She sewed the side of that boys head up and he went on home. She never talked bout how or where she learned to work on people.

After that day when folks got sick or got a cut plantin or doin she would say, "I got something for that." She would fix you up and say "You gon be alright."

Folks heard bout her from outside of Hideaway. It got to the place folks was knockin on her door in the late night. When the Sheriff found out she was taken bullets out of peoples legs, and carryin on, the law was always comin pass her house. Sister Basset knew when to say she helped somebody and when to say "ain't nobody been here."

We saw and heard for ourselves the way
she walked and prayed she would know quicker
then anybody if she was ever in any danger. We
never worried bout her and she never asked
anybody too. She did not fear strangers or the
law. It was her bizness. She took what people
could pay or traded her service for meat,
vegetables or any fixin they could do round her
place. God took care of June Basset and her
baby girl JuneNet.

Now here's where Smitty Reed come in the
story. He worked for his self and stayed pretty
much too his self. We use to see him from time
to time drivin his piece of truck lookin for work
or workin on a job. He was a carpenter that
could carve out, nail down, and put together
anything you wanted. He would help us out
from time to time in the church for a little bit of
nothing. He had a special gift.

He had heard bout some steady work up
North but cut his hand on a small job but did not
think it would mount to nothing. But it got worse.

Passin through our way he heard bout
Sister Bassett. It was a cold winter night, close
to Christmas, and Smitty Reed knocked on her
door. He knew by the look of his deep cut, he
needed special hands to take care of his badly
swollen infected hand.

She answered her door with her usual no fear, frown face and saw his hand long before she looked at him. The next mornin we saw Smitty's truck and knew where he was.

So you know some of us got to tellin one another what we thought was bein said and done in her house, from our visits over there. She asked Smitty to take a seat the way she do all her patients and she went to work. With his truck sittin there as long as it did we knew his illness must have been serious.

Mr. Finches knocked on her door cause he needed some oniment for a boil he had. He let some of us know Smitty waited too long to tend to his self and needed care throughout the night cause infection sat in and he had a fever. He told us Smitty was in her bed. That ain't nothin new, she has laid a many people on that bed and took care of them til they was healed.

We knew Sister Bassett was gon change that bandage every four hours, wipe his forehead, and sit by his side til his fever broke. Smitty was there goin on two days. We figured they had to be gettin to know each other with him stil bein weak and all.

Smitty probably wanted to know just like us, where she was from. Smitty was a proper talkin man, we could hear him say, "I know you are not from round here. Where are you and your baby girl from and how did you learn to doctor on people?"

We knew she was not in the fear anybody mood. Smitty bein the man he was she probably felt that she could trust him. We bet she pulled close up on him and got to talkin.

Smitty felt the need to share with a few of us from church way after he was well a little bit bout her.

He told us not to tell anybody. Now when you tell somebody not to tell something, you got to remember when you tell it, the best kept secrets are the one God only knows. But let me move on. She told Smitty she was from a small place in the mountains. Her father was white and her mother was black. Her father owned a general store and her mother worked for him. They did well, cause there was not a store for miles round.

"When her mother was not helpin out in his store she healed the sick. Sister Bassett just said her momma learned from her people and passed it on to her. Sister Bassett watched how gentle she was with people and how softly she spoke to them." Smitty said. "Her mother seemed to come alive when she was round the sick no matter her at-home struggles. She was calm and steady." We noticed that bout Sister Bassett.

She told Smitty her mother made her watch and listen and learn as she carefully put together the right herbs and create the right potions to heal the sick. She taught her what not to do to make sure people were not harmed or died by certain plants. She told Smitty her mother taught her how important it was to keep the knives and needles clean. She learned how to remove a bullet and sew up a hole with a steady hand. She stood side by side with her mother and assisted with helpin to deliver babies in the world. Sister Bassett told Smitty, it was as if it was her schoolin. While all this was happenin her father treated her mother as if she were his slave.

She watched as a child how her mother never complained bout the slaps he gave her across her face and the denial he had for her as his child.

Smitty said, "Her father was truly angry with himself for lyin with her mother and makin a baby girl that looked just like him. He was looked upon as poor white trash by his neighbors. He could not keep his secret from the world. He hated the sight of them but loved the control he had over them."

She told Smitty her father began to have sex with her by the time she was fifteen and made her watch as he beat her mother to death for tryin to stop him. She told Smitty there was no one to tell cause her father knew people would believe whatever he said.

Smitty said Sister Basset seemed to swell all up on the inside like she was on fire when she told this part. The same day her mother was buried her father had sex with her to celebrate. "She got pregnant and he got angry. But he did not know bout her anger. After her baby was born she took care of her child and continued to help him in his store as her mother did and healed the sick as best she could. She knew after the baby was born he would try her again," Smitty told us. He said Siter Bassett had no smile, no tears but a plan. That sho did explain her press–walkin self with no smile.

Smitty went on to say her mother taught her how to put herbs in food so they would not harm your stomach. So little by little she placed poisonous herbs in the food he ate. At first he said his stomach was hurtin and he complained of headaches. She knew the signs to look for when the herbs could cost him his life. She kept givin him the herbs til he got so sick he could not walk or keep any food on his stomach.

She ran the store and kept whatever money that came in til she had enough to leave with her baby. All the time Smitty was sharin this story with us we could understand more and more Sister Bassett's no-huggin ways.

I could not believe it when Smitty told us she prepared the necessary herbs for him to get well and placed it in a cup of hot tea and sat it next to his bed and did not leave a note. That's when she left to catch a better life for herself and that baby girl JuneNet.

That's when she and JuneNet got to Hideaway and bought that raggedy house and probably never looked back and wondered bout her father. That explains her prayer that Sunday in church. Sister Bassett did not want that life ever again.

Smitty did not go into no private time they had together. He just said they got to know each other better. We old women knew what it was to talk to a man in the late cold nights. He knew she was safe with him. We didn't tell Smitty we knew from our own settin–up-and-watchin ways bout her gift of seein people and knowin she could trust him the minute he steped in her doorway. He didn't have to say nothing. So if she laid beside Smitty she slept peacefully for a good while. The way he talked bout her, we had a feelin that Smitty was fallin in love. He called her a smart medicine women. He gave her that name just by how she tended to him. He told us he watched her soft warm hands move when she mashed, measured, and boiled leaves and plants in water and she knew just when to cool it, stir it up, bottle it, give it to you straight or serve it with something added to it. Smitty told us God gave him that woman and that child.

Now, let me tell you a little bit more bout Smitty Reed.

Smitty was a smart man. He didn't do no smokin or drinkin. He was a quiet pecan-colored man that used all the ings and eds at the end of his words. He talked real good. I don't mean slick, I mean like he was educated or something. Smitty was not real tall but tall enough where he could look down and stare in her eyes tenderly. You could tell he was a hard worker cause he had big strong arms and huge legs. He had a small waist so you could easily see how masculine he looked when his shirt was tucked tight down in his pants. He didn't smile much but when he did you saw pretty deep dimples.

We knew he had some rough times in his life tryin to live in the world that was a struggle for all people who looked like us, so he understood the scars she had. It wasn't long before

Smitty was able to move round. We saw him. I tell you he took that piece of house and tore it down piece by piece and rebuilt it. He was round there cuttin up, carvin out and sandin down wood makin fine chairs and any piece of furniture she needed to make life more comfortable for her. He was able to get work outside of Hideaway cause of his gift for makin things but he never stayed away no long time

Smitty stood up in the church and thanked God for sendin Sister Bassett to him. He promised God he would take care of her and her child for as long as he lived. He became a deacon and helped out in the church, did what he could for anybody with a smile. Sister Bassett had no frowns, no staleness; just sweetness all over her. They both raised JuneNet and loved on each other at the same time.

A couple of short years passed and Smitty died a mysterious death. He was found in the woods. Seems as though he had a deep cut on his head but the sheriff said he must have fallen somewhere. Our Hideaway town was just in a bad way. We couldn't figure out who would want to hurt him. Sister Bassett went deep into herself like she use to be, before she met Smitty. We couldn't comfort June and she would not let us.

Smitty had promised us not to share what he told us bout her daddy, mommy and her baby, some dark ugly sins have to stay covered up in them woods.

So we couldn't stop the half truths and made up lies that was flyin round in the air bout her life. Some folks said that old white daddy of hers found out where she was livin, with whom, and then killed him. He couldn't be happy livin with his shame so he didn't want her to have no happiness either. The sheriff in town didn't do much diggin round cause he said there wasn't no trail big enough to follow so he left Smitty's death a puzzle for us to put together.

Sister Bassett put that stale frown face back on. She soon dried her eyes, carried her child, packed her herbs, and took all her things and left Hideaway in his piece-a-truck shortly after Smitty died. We thought it was strange. The house was fixed up real nice. Smitty made sure the house was safe and sturdy for her and JuneNet. But Sister Bassett had a plan. We could tell it in the walk she had, as if somebody or something was pressin her to hurry up and get where she was goin.

13

Me and Randell

I told you bout all my neighbors who lived in Hideaway. Now I'm gon tell you bout me and Randell. He was only with me for a short while and then he left me. We first met in the Tiggs' juke joint.

It was the only time except Sunday and a funeral when we wore the best outfit we had. It was a time to look good and smell good. We danced and sweated clean out our clothes and hairdos. But you talk bout fun. Yes indeed! Those were some good times. We had a chance to forget bout them five days we had for a little while cause everybody knew Monday mornin was comin.

Anyway Randell walked over to me and said, "Doll Baby may I have this dance?" He held me real gentle like and looked me in the eyes when he talked to me not tryin to peep round the room at some other women's tail. We found a place for us to sit after we danced, just the two of us. He asked me did I want a drink, I said no thank you. I could tell by his smile he knew I wasn't a drinkin woman. We talked bout worldly things and gettin ahead in life. Even though we was livin through some rough times he didn't dream no small dreams. He wanted to have his own truckin bizness. He didn't spend no time complainin bout his boss man on that cotton farm.

He just said, "I work hard and I want something more outta life."

We went on seein one another like that for bout seven months. I saw a lot in him durin that time. He was a man's man. When he spoke the other men listened. He dressed neat all the time even when he wore work clothes. Tall, dark, handsome with muscles everywhere! He didn't cuss and act a fool. He did a lot of readin especially from the Bible and talked real plain like all the time. He wasn't scared of white folks so he didn't have to change up his words when they was round. Then the war came and he joined up.

We talked and made our plans to save our money and get married when he returned.

We did a lot of writin to each other. He told me he was tryin to learn all he could bout repairin trucks and big equipment cause them was skills he needed after the war. He was smart. He told me how Negro soldiers were treated even though they all was fightin the same war, for the same cause, for the same country but wasn't nothing equal. But he stayed steady and kept pressin.

I lived with my parents while he was in the service. I saved every penny, dime nickel, or dollar I could for four years while he was gon. He did the same. When he got out of the army we got married and stayed on with my parents til we was able to move. My husband bought a piece–a-truck so he could haul puck wood, cotton, and whatever he could tote to make ends meet. Now he didn't lose sight of his idea to have his own truckin bizness. Randell felt with what he learned in the service and goin to school to get a trade was the best way for us to get ahead.

He said, "I want to own the trucks and fix them too." Randell had his eyes set on a technical school. We only lived bout 80 miles from there. He applied for a GI loan to pay for his schoolin and books. Well, we prayed and we worked and we saved til that GI money came through.

Then we decided to try and get us our first home. I cleaned and cooked for a white family in town. Randell and I knew all bout them houses Mr. Cecil was either sellin or rentin to colored people. We knew bout the land bein cursed in his eyes and his sons movin out. I won't ever forget what Randell said to me: "Betteen, God don't curse no land that make people sin. Sin is something we choose to do." I told you he was smart.

Mr. Cecil knew me and my work. He had heard bout Randell and how hard he worked from the other white people round town. He was willin to sell us one of his houses but we had to put 200 dollars down. We had both been savin so we had it. Randell asked him could we give him half now and a little bit each month til we paid the down payment. Mr. Cecil told him yes. I asked Randell why he didn't want to give him all the money. He said, "If he knew we could give him the money right then he might ask for more. Then Mr. Cecil would want to know how we come by gettin it."

I told you he was smart.

After our payment Randell and I moved into our first home. We had to pay $65 every month. Just like our neighbors had a lot of work to do inside and out of their house we had to do the same. But we knew we had God so we moved forward. Lord knows there were days and nights, when we did not think that house was worth it. But when you set your mind on things beyond what you livin in and trust in God you can see your blessins one by one.

Randell went on to school three nights a week and worked the rest of the time haulin what he could. That went on bout a year. Randell got his certificate in auto mechanics. But he heard there was better work up North for black truck drivers.

We talked bout it along while, prayed bout it and came up with a plan. We didn't have no children. I ain't gon tell you we didn't try. But somehow or another I couldn't make babies. That wasn't something we spent a lot of time talkin bout with all that was goin on in the world round us. So we decided to love on each other just the two of us. Randell went on up North and tried to get work. We had saved enough to pay the rent for bout three months. If a job didn't come through he would be back. I would stay and keep workin til he could send for me. We knew it would not be a problem with Mr. Cecil to move out cause the house was in better shape than when we moved in it.

Randell got a job quick! He was haulin big heavy equipment from one construction site to another. He lived in a roomin house and came home on the week-ends when he didn't work overtime. I would have the grease hot and ready to cook us up some catfish by the time he got home. Randell would wash up and come back and sit at the table while I finished cookin. We ate and talked bout how everybody was doin but us. Somehow them plans for relocation got to be talked bout less and less. He went to bed and I washed the dishes. We made groceries on Saturday and we stopped to talk to friends we saw here and there. We'd go on home, eat something light and relax a bit, listen to the radio and looked at each other.

I would ask him what was he thinkin bout. He would always say, "I'm just thinkin bout my future." Now them words puzzled me, that it was his future now and not ours. But I didn't ask no questions. We laid out our Sunday clothes and went on to bed. We ate early after church cause he always wanted to leave before the traffic got bad. I packed him a lunch, he gave me the money to pay every bill we had and extra for whatever else that might come up. Randell gave me a kiss and a hug and left.

A year passed with the same week-end routine and I didn't ask no questions. Our love seemed to pass too. The last time Randell came home, I'll never forget it. He said, "I'm gon start sendin money home for the bills" and left. I didn't ask not one question. I let that man go on out that door and I closed it. He had nothing to say bout his nothingness to me. I wrote a letter and politely thanked him for the bill money. I asked him when was he comin home. He politely wrote me back and said, "I have grown out of you and my life is here now. I will continue to send money for the bills and a little extra for you to pay somebody to cut the grass and fix anything that needs fixin."

I was angry and hurt that he had grown out of me, when we planted so hard together. But I knew then, there was someone else that had the most precious part of him and I had the leftovers. I wanted to go up there and ask a lot of why, when and how he grew out of me questions but I didn't. I grew up hearin that if a man wonders off from home it must be something he not gettin.

So I spent days askin myself what did I not give him! I started drinkin myself drunk to sleep playin dreams over and over in my head tryin to backtrack and figure out where I lost him. I wore myself out cause I wasn't ready to give my anger my hurt and my cussin over to God yet and mad with Him cause He didn't give me no signs Randell was gon grow somewhere else.

I was young and not a bad lookin woman and didn't have nobody in the house. Some of the men folk in the church offered to comfort me when Randell left. There was one I allowed to do just that! But guess what? That didn't give me no peace.

A year had almost passed. The bill money was the only part of Randell I had at that point and I took it.

I never left home without my sadness and my self pity. I didn't take it out on nobody or shared it. Even on Sunday, I went to church, and did not ask or thank God for nothing! I was just angry. I did not want to talk to God, in His house!

Ain't that something?

But one Sunday on a pretty fall day Randell brought his other half to our home while I was at church. Now, I'm not gon lie to you. Randell never put her in my face but other folks met her and came back and told me. Randell left me a note and said he came to get his gun and some tools he had. I was hotter than hell so it was good I was not home when he and her came by.

But I couldn't be stil. I didn't take my Sunday clothes off. But I changed and put on my work shoes. It was a beautiful day so I went for a walk in the woods. Tears would not come so I kept walkin. I thought bout Randell some more. He truly found no fault in his self. He did not think he was a hoe-ish man. Randell did not beat me, or disrespect me in front of people. I had to remember what he told me. "Betteen, the land our house was built on did not cause people to sin, people sin cause they choose to."

I kept walkin and I thought some more.

He was a man who believed because he had worked hard and provided for me he had the right to leave me, plant somewhere else and enjoyed his sin cause he chose to!

I just stopped and jumped and called on Jesus like I had never done before. I asked God to take me and cover me up deep in the woods. I told God, "Please take my heart and wrap it up with your love so can't nobody hurt me." I got on my knees on the cool ground and dug my hands in the dirt askin God to forgive me for forgettin. He woke me up, and breathed fresh newness on me not, Randell. I thanked God for His mercy when I refused to allow Him to comfort me. I got up with dirt in my hands pleadin with God to help me move and sow new seeds.

I didn't want to stay stuck ponderin over a garden that would not grow. I had to find my own new do with God.

As I walked back home I realized I was not capable of fixin Randell. Whatever his needs or wants were, they were between him and God. I had to get ready and prepare for my own bloomin. I could keep workin every day and not complain bout the rent money I received every month from Randell. I thought bout what I wanted to do with me. I had no children no husband at home and wasn't a bad lookin woman. I had some time on my hands. I decided to go to school. Yes I did!

I always wanted to dress nice and work in an office somewhere.

I kept my day job cleanin for folks but I took classes at night in English, math and secretarial skills like typin. I was real good at it. When I finished night school I got me a job. I worked at a black funeral home part time. I did some typin and assisted people with their plan for their loved ones funeral. I enjoyed helpin people. I met a lot of interestin people. I did some travelin and went to some dances but I never strayed far from God.

Somebody had told Randell I was lookin good and he came by every now and then to our place in Hideaway to see how I was doin. I was never rude but I never had much time to spend with him. He noticed the change in me but never felt it necessary to explain his new seed plantin.

I saved my little money for a good while. I was in my early fifties by then. I decided to move. I was gettin up in age and I wanted to live in town where I could get round and not depend on no body. I found me this small one bedroom, real cute and just right for me. The only somebody who can stay here and come and go when he pleases is God. I contacted Randell and told him my movin out date and, he told me he was movin back in. I guess he was gon surprise me with his comin back home. I didn't let that information cause me to ask God was this one of them   sit-and-wait-and-see-what-Randell-gon-do. We ain't had a sit down meetin on why and how in all that time and I did not need one then. I kept my movin plans. I did not want to try and figure out how Rendell's garden was growin.

He didn't wait to move in after I left; he arrived on my movin day early that mornin. He didn't knock, he came on in like he lived there. We didn't meet each other half way in the livin room floor with no hug or nothing. He nodded at me while lookin round the room, not at me, but like he was inspectin something. We didn't discuss what furniture was stayin and what was goin.

I said, "Hello how you doin." He didn't say nothing, I could see why. His hair had thinned, and what hair he had was mostly gray. He looked tired and worn. I knew then it was not gon be a let-me-explain-to-you-Betteen-why-I'm-back. I felt based on what I knew bout a man that left me and comes back home sick, the woman he was with didn't take to caterin to no man she got to nurse. This was not the time for me to clap my hands and laugh at him. I was not gon be a devil. I politely said, "Thank you Randell for takin care of me in your own way."

"You welcome," he said, stil not even lookin at me. But I wanted to have one more good look at him, one more time. He was thin, weak lookin but his clothes stil neat. I went over and kissed that man on his check. I don't think it was love for him, I felt sorry for him. Randell grabbed my hand and held it tight. "I'm gon be by myself, you can stay if you like," he said easin to a chair to sit in, but not lookin in my face the whole time he said that one sentence.

I wanted to cuss real good. I moved over to that chair where he was sittin and stood with my hands on my hips lookin down hard on him so hard, playin in my head right quick bout them why–me? nights, drunk, mad with God, tryin to explain to myself why he left me. All I could get out my mouth was, "Why Randell"?

He did not hurry up and give me an answer and I knew if I walked away he would not give me one, so I stood. He cleared his throat. "You never questioned what I did, or nagged me bout nothin." I heard what he said but he was talkin real low. I asked him to speak up. He cleared his throat again and said,"You never asked bout my goin and doin, you never nagged me. I'm a man, it was something I felt I needed."

I wanted to cut him. But I let him talk.

"I made sure I took care of you. We had no children and I never had to worry bout you. You are not a needy woman Betteen. You worked hard Betteen and you valued what we had done together. For a while I enjoyed comin home to you and the way you took care of the house and always ready to greet me and everything was always in place. But she had a way of makin me feel like I was the center of her life. I loved that and I needed that; I felt I had earned that. I didn't have no nights when I could not sleep and I never asked God to forgive me for how I lived up there or down here with you. It just got to the place that I liked how it made me feel."

Now the whole time he was talkin he stil wouldn't set eyes on me.

Those old feelins of bitterness and self-pity wanted to creep up on me. So, I wanted to cuss and fight. I was not concerned bout his sickly self. All I could think of was how important he thought of himself and didn't feel the need to discuss his selfish behavior with God. I could see and hear for myself, Randell could never tell me he was sorry. I didn't want to be round a man who found nothing wrong with bein wicked and thought it was alright with God. I never ever thought of myself as bein better then Randell cause it took me a good while to let go of all that hatred towards him to understand that the blessins God had for me wasn't comin as long as I wished something evil to happen to him. I had to go. I gently got my hands off my hips and my eyes off Randell.

When I had everything packed and ready to go. I left Randell sittin in that chair. I didn't ask him if he needed any help with his move cause I was sure Randell already had a come back home growin plan, it just didn't include me.

I found some real kind people to help me move my things and load it up real neat in their truck. When I saw that I didn't forget anything, cause Lord knows I did not want to come back, I got to the door and looked back at Randell and told him, "Take care of yourself and thank you for everything."

I did not wait for an answer. I felt complete. I had learned from prayer and Bible study that forgivin others who mistreat you comes first and the forgettin of how they mistreated you comes in time with constant prayer.

I told my neighbors that were stil livin there, I was leavin. We hugged each other while a few was peekin in the doorway at Randell. I had no news to give. When I got in my car I drove slowly round the curve lookin and thinkin bout my neighborhood. I smiled with tears not of bitterness but of thankfulness.

But right before I made that turn at the foot of the path, I had to stop where the Big Mamma tree was standin. I got out the car, took a minute to walk round and rub my hands across her big waist. I laughed and clapped my hands out loud shakin my head thinkin to myself, this land was never cursed and never caused us to sin.

That was never God's plantin plan for us.

We all were in a small community together each havin our own testimony we could share with somebody. It did not matter what type or how heavy our sadness was or for how long you carried it, it was bout us askin God to remove it.

There were those of us who could not see we were destroyin ourselves. Some of us found no fault in our life and did see the need not to change. For those that stayed for a short while and could see they had to grow somewhere else stepped out and moved with faith. Some of us were able to take the darkest disappointment in our lives, live and pray through it, to find peace we never thought we would have. Some of us did not always look at our victories, big or small as the power to go on and believe God would continue to fill us up time after time if we needed it.

But God was there all the time. I think sometimes God walked real slow in Hideaway waitin on us cause we wasn't sure bout movin forward in His well and His way.

For me to tell you why God chose us to dwell in that place at that time is His mystery. I know he provided us with a place to live and worship all in one. He gave us what we needed every day in a secret place called Hideaway.

www.ingramcontent.com/pod-product-compliance
Lightning Source LLC
Chambersburg PA
CBHW030633130626
46552CB00002B/828